NINE LIVES
DAISY, BUTTERCUP AND WEED

LUCY DANIELS
Nine Lives
Daisy, Buttercup and Weed

Illustrated by Bill Geldart

*Hodder
Children's
Books*

a division of Hodder Headline

Special thanks to Heather Maisner

Copyright © 1999 Working Partners Limited
Created by Working Partners Limited, London W6 0QT
Text copyright © 1999 Working Partners Limited
Illustrations copyright © 1999 Bill Geldart
Cover illustration by Anne Sharp

First published in Great Britain in 1999
by Hodder Children's Books

A Catalogue record for this book is available from the British Library

ISBN 0 340 73621 6

Typeset by Avon Dataset Ltd, Bidford-on-Avon, Warks

Printed and bound in Great Britain by
The Guernsey Press Co. Ltd, Guernsey, Channel Isles

Hodder Children's Books
a division of Hodder Headline
338 Euston Road
London NW1 3BH

For Figaro and Mist

Nine Lives

Bracken is a large tortoiseshell cat who
lives with the Bradman family on Liberty
Street. Bracken lives a comfortable life,
and spends much of her time snoozing
away in her basket in the Bradmans'
house.

Mr Bradman – Dad – used to be a lawyer,
but he gave up this career for his real passion
– gardening. He found Bracken abandoned

in a skip two years ago when she was just a tiny kitten.

Mrs Bradman – Mum – is a bank manager. Unlike Mr Bradman, she loves her indoor office job.

Elsie Jennings – or Gran – is Mrs Bradman's mum. She lives a few doors away on Liberty Street. She may be over 65, but Elsie has loads of get up and go and enjoys being with children. That's why she loves her job as the local lollipop lady!

Tom Bradman is thirteen years old, and has an early morning job as a paperboy. He and his younger sister, Ellie, love animals. They always make a big fuss of Bracken and their six year-old Golden Retriever, Lottie.

Ellie Bradman is ten years old. She's always coming up with brilliant plans and ideas – which is just as well . . . because earlier this year Bracken had her first litter. She became the proud mum of nine assorted bundles of fur . . .

★ ★ ★

Nine kittens; nine very different lives. The Bradmans know they can't keep the kittens but they're determined that all nine go to the very best homes – homes to suit each, very special personality . . .

Daisy

1

"I'm really worried about you," Mel's mum said to her, as Mel and her friend Ben ran in from the garden. "You've nearly finished all your medicine and you're still coughing."

"I'm fine," Mel said quickly. "I only cough when I come into a warm room from outside." Her mum had kept her off school last week, and she'd been bored and lonely.

She didn't want to spend another week off sick. She preferred to be at school, out and about with her friends.

"If you're still coughing tomorrow, I'm taking you back to the doctor," Mrs Barnett said sternly. "You know we have to take special care of your chest. Now go and have a rest and stop rushing around."

"OK, Mum. But I'm all right. Really I am," Mel said, as she and Ben made their way upstairs to play on her computer. Mel had a weak chest and was prone to bronchitis ever since she'd been very ill with pneumonia when she was little. Her mum always worried that her coughs and colds would turn into bronchitis or – worse – pneumonia again.

Daisy, Mel's small white kitten, was curled up on Mel's bed. She opened her pale blue eyes as they came into the room.

Mel sat down and stroked her. "I'm really worried about you," Mel said, shaking her head. "Why don't you purr or miaow like other cats?"

Daisy looked back at her. *You've no need to worry*, she wanted to tell Mel. *I love it here with you. It's much better than at the Bradmans' house with my eight brothers and sisters all making loads of noise. I like being quiet. It's just the way I am.*

Mel stroked Daisy's soft, thick coat and Daisy rolled onto her back. She was the quietest of Bracken's kittens. The Bradmans, who owned Bracken, had told Mel that Daisy hadn't made a sound since the day she was born. And she'd been living with Mel and

her parents for two months now, but she still hadn't purred or miaowed.

"I don't know how you're feeling if you don't make any noise," Mel said. "Maybe you're really miserable!"

"She probably is," Ben said, looking away from the computer screen for a second. "Because you keep fussing over her all the time!"Ben lived a few streets away. His mum and Mel's mum, Mrs Barnett, were best friends and he often came back to Mel's house after school, while his mum was still at work.

"You don't know what you're talking about," Mel said to Ben. "How would you like it if your dog never barked or . . . or . . .?"

"If you stopped talking for a moment or two . . ." Ben added quickly, "I'd manage to get a word in edgeways and—"

Mel stood up and threw a cushion at him. Ben managed to dodge it.

"You don't understand," Mel continued. "I mean what if there's something wrong with her?"

There's nothing wrong with me. Daisy looked up. *I just don't want to talk.*

"But you know there's nothing wrong with her. It's not as if she's ill or anything. You've taken her to about six vets," insisted Ben.

"Two vets actually," Mel said crossly. "And I know that. But what would happen if I lost her or she got in trouble? She wouldn't be able to let anyone know. Because nobody would be able to hear her, would they?"

I hadn't thought of that, Daisy said to herself, feeling a little bit worried.

"Then don't let her get into trouble," Ben replied. "You certainly like to worry, don't you?" he added.

Mel stroked Daisy's white coat and stared at her beautiful blue eyes. "Maybe I do worry too much," she whispered to the kitten, "but I'd just love to hear your voice."

It was the following day, and Mel was really worried now. She had come home from school, opened the front door and called for Daisy as she always did. Usually Daisy came running to greet her. But today there was no pitter patter of feet on the kitchen floor. Today there was complete silence.

"Daisy! I'm home!" Mel called again, kicking off her shoes in the hall, then making her way to the sitting-room. Perhaps Daisy was asleep on the sofa or stretched out in a patch of sunshine on the carpet. Mel went to look. But there was no sign of her.

"Daisy! Daisy! Where are you?" Mel shouted, running up the stairs. She flung open her bedroom door. But Daisy wasn't in there either. Mel went on looking – in her mum and dad's room, and then in the bathroom. But Daisy wasn't anywhere.

Mel wiped her forehead and peeled off her sweater. She'd been feeling hot all day. Now she was sweating. She hurried downstairs and into the kitchen, to tell her mum.

But the kitchen was empty. Mel looked out of the window and saw her mum out in the garden, hanging up washing. The washing machine made a whirring noise. Her mum had put in another load. Things were whirling round and round in there. White things!

Mel watched in horror. *What if one of those white things is Daisy, caught up in the washing?* she thought.

"Mum . . . Quick!" Mel cried in a panic. "We have to stop the machine!" But Mrs Barnett didn't hear her.

Mel rushed over to the machine. She needed to stop it – and quickly! She saw a button marked "stop" and pressed it. The machine went quiet. Then she tried to open the door. But it was stuck fast! Mel pulled and pulled.

"What on earth are you doing?" Mel's mum asked, opening the back door and hurrying into the kitchen.

"Mum, quick," said Mel. "Daisy's in there!"

"That's ridiculous," Mrs Barnett said, putting down the empty washing basket.

"Of course she's not in there. I'd have seen her."

"But what if you didn't?" Mel said, worriedly. "She's as white as the sheets and if she was caught in a pillow or a duvet cover, you wouldn't have noticed her, would you?" Mel kept looking through the glass door of the washing machine.

"Of course I would. I would have felt her and . . ."

"But she isn't anywhere in the house so she must be in there. Please Mum, help me!" Mel was starting to panic now, and began to cough and splutter.

Mrs Barnett looked worriedly at Mel. "Oh, all right then – if it will make you feel better," she said. Quickly she reached under the sink and pulled out a screwdriver. Then she took a small panel from the front of the machine, and switched the door lock off.

Mel yanked open the door and began to pull out the washing. "Thank goodness the machine hadn't had time to fill up with water yet!" she said. "Daisy would have drowned!"

She shook out the white T-shirts. Then she felt all round the inside of a big white duvet, pushing her hands into the corners. She did the same with the white pillowcases. Her mum got down on her hands and knees and helped. But Daisy wasn't there.

"Thank goodness," Mel sighed. For a moment she relaxed. But then she thought, *If Daisy isn't in the washing machine – where is she?* She dashed out of the room.

"What about this mess, Mel?" her mother called after her.

But Mel was busy looking in all the rooms again, calling, "Daisy! Daisy! Here, Daisy."

Daisy heard Mel calling from far away. She opened her eyes and blinked. *Where am I?* It was very dark and she had no idea where she was. She lifted up her head but it knocked against something hard.

"Daisy, Daisy, where are you?" she heard Mel calling.

Here. Daisy opened her mouth but nothing came out. She tried to reach out and make a noise by scratching but she couldn't manage it. She was cramped up in a very small space. *I wish I hadn't gone exploring*, she thought. *I don't like it here. Please find me, Mel.*

Mel was on the landing, feeling the narrow space behind the dresser, when the doorbell rang.

"Mel, do you want to come out and play?" Ben shouted up the stairs when Mrs Barnett opened the door.

"I can't," she shouted back. "Daisy's disappeared. Come and help me find her."

"Cats don't disappear," Ben said, climbing the stairs two at a time.

Daisy could just hear what they were saying. *You're right there*, she thought. *I'm not too far away.*

"They just like being on their own sometimes," he continued.

But Mel disagreed, "Well, this cat has disappeared," she said. "Mum was out most of the day and now I can't find her. Oh Ben, what am I going to do?" She began to cough again.

Mel sounded like she might cry and this made Daisy feel really bad. She wriggled around in her tight, dark space and wished that she could jump out and comfort Mel.

"Have you looked in the cellar?" Ben asked.

"No, I didn't think of that," Mel said. "But maybe Mum went down there this morning and Daisy ran in after her. Come on!"

Mel raced downstairs, found the key hanging in the kitchen, and opened the cellar door. "Daisy. Here, Daisy," she called. She tried to switch on the light but it didn't work.

"We'll have to go down in the dark," Ben said. "Follow me."

Clinging to each other, they slowly made their way down the steps. It was damp and cold in the cellar and the room was piled high with boxes of old clothes, tools, camping equipment and all sorts of things nobody wanted any more.

"Daisy," they called. "We're here. Come out."

Daisy heard them calling and thought, *If only I could move.* She tried to wriggle and stretch but there wasn't any room. Hurry up and find me Mel, she said to herself. I don't like being in this dark, cramped place. It's scary.

Mel pulled out boxes and felt behind the ones that were too heavy to move. Cobwebs brushed against her face but she kept on pulling and pushing. She was shivering now, as well as coughing.

Ben reached up for a box and it toppled over, crashing to the floor. Hundreds of tiny screws spilled out, rolling across the floor. They couldn't see in the dark to pick them up, and anyway, they didn't have time.

Mel got down on her hands and knees and felt around behind another big box. Suddenly her fingers felt something soft and furry. Her heart lifted. "She's here!"

At the same moment her mother shouted down the stairs. "What are you two up to? What on earth was that noise? Come upstairs at once."

"We're looking for Daisy," Ben began.

"And we knocked over a box and everything spilled out and . . ."

"I've found her!" Mel shouted out. "Only she isn't moving!"

2

Slowly Mel carried Daisy up the stairs, her heart filled with fear. She closed her eyes when she reached the light, too frightened to look at what was in her arms.

"That's not Daisy," Ben said, laughing. "It's your old teddy. The one with only one eye."

Mel opened her eyes with relief and looked down at her old teddy. Its thick fur had felt just like Daisy's!

"And Daisy definitely isn't down there," Mrs Barnett said firmly. "We always keep the cellar door locked. And it hasn't been opened for weeks."

"Then where is she?" Mel asked, coughing and starting to feel hot again. "I've looked everywhere!"

"What about the airing cupboard?" Ben asked. "Did you look there? Our cat sometimes goes to sleep in ours, if someone leaves it open by mistake."

They rushed upstairs to the bathroom and threw open the airing cupboard. It was dark and cramped, and piled high, with clean washing. They pulled the washing out onto the bathroom floor. But there was no sign of Daisy.

Then Ben pointed to the window. "It's open," he said. "Maybe she climbed out."

"Oh no!" Mel wailed.

"Hang on, we don't know she got out," Ben said.

But Mel was tearing downstairs again, panting and coughing. "Where are my shoes?" she shouted to her mother.

"Slow down," Mrs Bennett said. "You can't go rushing around like this. That cough is getting worse," she said anxiously.

"But I have to go and look outside for Daisy," Mel spluttered. "She could have wandered off and got hurt. And maybe she can't find her way back home again."

"We'll all go looking together," Mel's mum said. "But first you must take your medicine and—"

Her words were interrupted by a screech of brakes in the street outside, followed by a loud crash.

"Oh, no!" Mel cried in horror. "That could be Daisy!" She pulled open the front door and ran out into the street without even putting on her shoes.

With her heart pounding in her ears, she headed towards the place where a car had crashed into a wall.

A circle of people had gathered around the car. Mrs Woods from Number 6 was leaning forward talking to the driver with her young daughter Monica beside her.

What if Daisy's under the car? Mel drew in her breath, then bent down to look under the wheels. It was dark under there and, at first, Mel couldn't see anything.

Gradually her eyes got used to the dim light. But all she could see was Monica's face staring at her from the other side of the car. "What are you looking for?" the little girl asked.

"My white kitten," Mel said. "Have you seen her?"

"No, but . . ." Monica rolled her eyes and paused.

"But what?" Mel asked.

"Well, that driver told my mum she saw something small and white run in front of the car. That's why she swerved and crashed and—"

"Oh no!" Mel cried. She spun around in panic and then headed off towards the nearest front garden. *Poor Daisy must be terrified, she thought. She must be hiding somewhere near here. But where?*

It had been raining on and off for weeks and all the plants had grown so quickly that the gardens looked like mini jungles with their long lush leaves. Daisy could be anywhere in any one of them.

"Daisy, please come out," she begged. "Daisy, please show me where you are."

Something white jumped up out of the bushes and scurried through the plants. Mel crashed after it.

"What are you doing? Why are you in my flowerbeds?" a voice shouted after her.

But Mel didn't call back. She didn't want to frighten Daisy. "Here, Daisy. Here," she whispered. "Come to me. Please come to me."

Suddenly, the white something Mel had been chasing leapt out at great speed, almost knocking her over. It was white and furry like Daisy but bigger – and it was yapping furiously. It was Mrs Edwards' poodle, Perry.

"That's it! That's what ran in front of my car," the driver of the blue car shouted.

"There you are," Mel's mum said, hurrying

over and wrapping a coat around her shoulders. "You haven't even got your shoes on, and you're shivering."

"Oh, Mum," Mel coughed. "I felt sure I'd found Daisy. Now I've got to start all over again."

"No. First, you must come home and put on some warm clothes," her mother said firmly.

"But Mum . . ."

"No buts. I really am worried about you, love," Mrs Barnett said seriously. "You don't look at all well."

Ben was waiting by the open front door. He gave her a strange look. "You've gone all red, Mel," he said.

"Go and find your warmest sweater," said her mum. "And change your socks – those ones are filthy now. Then we'll decide what to do."

Shivering and coughing and still calling for her kitten, Mel walked slowly upstairs with Ben.

Daisy heard a door open. She heard

someone coughing and sniffing and calling her name. "Daisy! Daisy! Where are you?"

It was Mel's voice but it didn't sound like Mel because her voice was croaky.

Daisy wriggled round in her small space. *What can I do to get her attention?* she wondered. She tried to stretch out and scratch at a piece of wood but she hit her head again on something above her. She opened her mouth to miaow – but as usual, nothing came out. *Now I really wish I could talk*, she thought. *I could be in here forever!*

Mel was banging doors and cupboards. Tears were rolling down her cheeks now. *It isn't fair, she thought. If only Daisy could miaow, I'd know where to look for her. She could be lost forever!* Sniffing, Mel pulled open her sock drawer – then gasped.

At the same moment Daisy's dark space was filled with light and she stared up at a tear-stained but familiar face.

"Daisy!" Mel shrieked. She lifted her kitten out of the drawer and clutched her against her chest.

"Brilliant!" shouted Ben, rushing over. "I knew we'd find her!"

"You silly thing, how did you get in there?" Mel asked, nuzzling close to Daisy.

Daisy rubbed her face against Mel's chin. *Because, you silly thing,* she wanted to say, *you shoved the drawer shut while I was exploring. And I couldn't let you know I was in here and so I just had to wait and hope you'd find me.*

Mel danced round the room with Daisy, singing croakily, "I've found her! I've found her!" Then she flopped down on the bed, still holding Daisy tight. Her heart was beating very fast now, and she was finding it a little hard to breathe. Her face felt wet and sticky.

"Are you sure you're all right?" Ben asked, looking at her strangely again. "You've gone all white, now."

"I'm fine now that I've found Daisy," Mel croaked.

Me too, thought Daisy. *I must have been in that drawer all day.* She reached up to lick Mel's chin. *Only now I feel very hungry,* she thought as she wriggled out of Mel's arms

and ran lightly down the stairs to the kitchen. But her bowl was empty. *Now what?* she wondered.

Mrs Barnett was in front of the cooker tossing some food in a pan. A wonderful smell filled the room. But Mel's mum hadn't realised Daisy was there.

Daisy walked over to Mrs Barnett and rubbed against her legs. "So there you are, Daisy," Mel's mum said, swinging round and smiling at her. "Thank goodness you've turned up again. You had us all really worried."

She bent down to stroke Daisy's head. "I suppose you're hungry after your adventure," she said, taking a half-finished tin of cat food out of the fridge and emptying it into Daisy's bowl. "If only you'd miaow when you want something," she said fondly, watching the snowy white kitten falling over herself to get to the food.

"If she could miaow I'd have found her ages ago," Mel said, running into the kitchen, wheezing. "Mum, she was in my top drawer all day long. We have to take her to another vet. We have to, otherwise things like this will keep happening."

Daisy stopped eating. *Oh no, not another vet!* she thought. *They push me and poke me and then say I'm OK. And I am OK, really I am.*

"They all say she'll find her voice one day," Mrs Barnett said gently.

But Mel was insistent. "Please mum. Please," she croaked. She was shivering a lot and her teeth were chattering.

"Where's Ben?" Mrs Barnett asked.

"He's gone to watch TV in the sitting-room, now we've found Daisy," Mel replied, watching the kitten as she started to gobble down her food again.

"OK," Mrs Barnett said. "It's Saturday tomorrow so there's no school. I'll make an appointment with the vet – if you go to bed straight away."

Half an hour later, Ben had gone home and Mel lay in bed with a hot lemon drink. Daisy was curled up beside her.

Her mum came in to say goodnight. "How are you feeling, love?" she asked.

"I'm fine," Mel whispered. She was beginning to lose her voice. "Except I can't speak!"

Me too, Daisy thought.

"What a pair!" Mrs Barnett exclaimed. "You're almost as white and quiet as each other." She shook her head and closed the door, mumbling to herself. "I'm worried about you both."

Brrring! The alarm clock burst into life.

Daisy opened one eye, then shut it again. *I don't want to get up yet*, she thought. The sun was peeping through a gap in the curtains making a nice, warm patch on the duvet.

Mel rolled over, coughed and stretched out her arm to turn off the alarm. Then she gave Daisy a cuddle before snuggling down under the bedcovers again.

Then Mel's mum opened the bedroom door and asked, "Are you awake, Mel?" She saw Mel wriggling about under the bedcovers. "It's time to get up if we're going to take Daisy to the vet – but I don't want you to get out of bed unless you're well enough."

"I'm fine!" Mel whispered. She wasn't doing to miss out on taking Daisy to the vet's just because she felt a little bit ill!

"OK then," said Mrs Barnett. "If you're sure . . ." She closed the door again and went downstairs.

Oh no, are we really going to the vet? Daisy was dismayed. *I hoped everyone would forget about that.*

Mel forced herself awake, rubbing her eyes and stretching. She sat up and clambered out of bed. "Come on Daisy. We've got to get ready," she whispered.

She was about to open the door and go to the bathroom when she stopped and clutched at her forehead mumbling, "Oh dear, I feel dizzy." And then she fell to the floor.

3

Startled, Daisy looked at Mel lying in a heap. Mel, what's the matter? Daisy ran up and nudged her shoulder. But Mel didn't move.

Please Mel, get up. Or at least open your eyes! Daisy licked Mel's chin and nuzzled against her. But still Mel didn't stir.

What shall I do? Daisy wondered. *I need to get help.*

Downstairs she could hear footsteps on the

wooden floor and doors opening and shutting. The smell of toast wafted up the stairs.

Help! she wanted to shout. Somebody please come and help Mel! But as usual no sound came out.

She ran to the door and scratched at it. She could hear Mel's mum and dad talking downstairs, but they were too far away to hear her.

Daisy ran up and down beside Mel looking at her and worrying.

Mel just lay where she was, her face white and her chest going up and down as she breathed.

Oh dear, there's something really wrong with Mel and nobody knows about it, except me, Daisy realised. *And I can't help her because I can't speak so nobody can hear me. Somehow, I HAVE to speak!*

Daisy stood by the door and took a deep breath. She opened her mouth wide and, strained with all her might, thinking, *Help! Help!*

Daisy heard a little tiny squeak that startled her. *Who made that noise?* she wondered and she looked around the room. But there was no one there apart from Mel, who lay on the floor with her eyes shut.

Downstairs the doorbell rang and Daisy heard Mel's mum open the door to the postman.

Come up here, you must come up here. Daisy said in her head. She opened her mouth, took another breath, and tried again to make a sound . . .

Mrs Barnett closed the front door and was on her way back to the kitchen carrying a parcel when she heard a strange noise. She stopped and frowned. What on earth is that? she wondered. It seems to be coming from Mel's bedroom. She dropped the parcel and ran upstairs.

As she opened Mel's bedroom door, Daisy ran at her, miaowing and miaowing desperately.

"You clever girl," Mel's mum began. "You can miaow!"

Then she stopped as she caught sight of

Mel on the floor and realised why Daisy was upset. "Quick, Andrew!" she shouted to Mel's dad. "Come quickly!"

Ten minutes later Mel's mum drove off to the hospital with Mel lying on the back seat of the car, while Daisy watched from the sitting-room window.

"I want to come too," she miaowed but everyone was too busy to listen to her.

Daisy turned to Mel's dad who was putting on his coat. She jumped down and rubbed against his legs. "I'm so worried about Mel," she miaowed. "I want to go with her to the hospital."

Mr Barnett bent down to stroke Daisy, smiling. "You found your voice and came to Mel's rescue, and now you can't keep quiet!" He turned and picked up the cat carrier that Mrs Barnett had got ready to take Daisy to the vet's.

But Daisy backed away, arching her back. "I don't need to go to the vet's now," she miaowed.

Mel's dad suddenly realised what was wrong. He stroked her gently and said, "Don't worry, Daisy. I'm not taking you to the vet. I'm taking you to Ben's house."

Oh, that's not so bad, Daisy thought. *At least Ben is Mel's best friend. He'll understand.*

Mel's dad lifted Daisy into the cat carrier and she curled up on one of Mel's old cotton T-shirts that he had put there as a blanket.

Mel's dad closed the front door behind him and set off along the street with Daisy. She peeped through the slits in the cat carrier and from time to time she practised her new voice. "Hello, hello," she miaowed to everyone she saw.

She loved the way everyone turned around to see who was making so much noise. *Nobody really noticed me before*, she thought. *Now everyone is looking my way.*

As they passed the corner shop, Daisy saw Elsie Jennings. She was the local lollipop lady, who helped children across the road when they were on their way to school. But it was Saturday today, so Mrs Jennings didn't have her big white coat on — or her big lollipop-shaped sign with her.

Daisy let out an extra-loud miaow. "Hello, Mrs Jennings!" she called.

"Remember me? I'm Bracken's little white kitten." Mrs Jennings had known Daisy since the day she was born, because Daisy's mum, Bracken, lived with Mrs Jennings' daughter.

Mrs Jennings was so surprised that she almost dropped her bag of shopping. "Well I never," she exclaimed. "Daisy can speak!"

"Not only that," Mel's dad told her. "Daisy's voice saved the day." And he told her all about how Daisy had raised the alarm for Mel.

All day and during the night, Daisy worried about Mel. *Please, Mel, please get better*, she said to herself. *Please come home soon.*

She was so nervous that she couldn't stop miaowing. She miaowed when the doorbell went and she miaowed when the telephone rang. She miaowed whenever anybody left the room and she miaowed whenever Ben's dog, Flip, came anywhere near her. She made so much noise that everybody wished she would be silent again.

"I thought you said she was a quiet little kitten" Ben's mum said.

"She was," Ben replied. "Mel won't believe it when she hears her." At the mention of Mel's name, Daisy miaowed even louder.

Late the following morning, Ben's doorbell rang. It was Mrs Barnett, looking very happy. "Mel's home again now, and she's going to be fine," she told Ben and his parents.

"Hurrah!" Daisy miaowed and the noise she made was the happiest and loudest yet.

"Great!" said Ben.

Mrs Barnett nodded, smiling. "The hospital says that as long as she rests and takes her medicine, she won't become really ill with bronchitis this time. So I've come to collect Daisy."

"Can I come and see Mel later?" Ben asked.

"Come round after lunch," Mrs Barnett suggested.

As Mel's mum carried her home, Daisy got more and more excited. She couldn't wait to let Mel hear her new voice. "Hurry up, hurry up," she miaowed.

"Ssh Daisy," Mrs Barnett laughed. "Don't you do anything now but miaow?"

"I can't stop," Daisy replied. "I have to see Mel."

As soon as Mrs Barnett let Daisy out of her cat carrier, she fled up the stairs to Mel's

bedroom and sprang onto Mel's bed. "I'm so pleased to see you!" she miaowed loudly.

"Daisy," Mel whispered, "Is that really you, making all that noise?" She gave Daisy a hug. "I've waited so long to hear your voice! I'm so happy!"

"I'm happy too," Daisy replied. She snuggled down in the duvet, as close to Mel as she could get.

And then Daisy began to make another noise – one that she hadn't made yet, one that she'd been saving especially for the person she loved the most . . . It was the loudest purr that Mel had ever heard!

Buttercup

1

I wonder if this is a good time to have a nap? Buttercup yawned. *I'm soooo tired!*

She nosed open the cat-flap and looked warily into the kitchen. "Hurrah! It's empty," she purred to herself. Buttercup squeezed through, ran over to her basket in the corner and curled up on her blanket.

She was just beginning to doze off when the door flew open and baby Lee came running into the kitchen. He was holding a model aeroplane in one hand and shouting, "Mine, mine – MINE!" at the top of his voice.

"It ISN'T yours!" Freddie, his nine-year-old brother cried, thundering in behind him. "Give it here! You'll break it! And you've already broken my computer game!" He tried to grab the aeroplane from the toddler.

"No, mine!" Lee repeated, running round the table and knocking over a chair.

"Give it back NOW!" Freddie shouted, gaining ground.

"MINE!" Lee shrieked back. Then he fell backwards, toppling into Buttercup's basket – with Freddie on top of him.

Buttercup sprang out of the basket just in time and ran under the kitchen table. *Another nap ruined!* she thought wearily. *This is too much! I feel as if I haven't had a proper sleep since the day I was born!*

When Buttercup was born at the Bradmans' house, she'd shared her mum, Bracken, with eight brothers and sisters.

Bracken had kept them all in order — but still, it had often been very crowded and noisy.

Buttercup had looked forward to going to her new home, where she would have some peace and quiet. But the Chapman family, who had chosen her, were even bigger and noisier than the Bradmans!

There was Mr and Mrs Chapman and their five children — Freddie, Clare, Jim, Gilly and baby Lee — and Gran and Granddad, who lived downstairs in the basement flat. Buttercup loved them all, but they never left her alone! *I really do need a few moments to myself*, she thought, as she hid under the table. She decided to give herself a wash while she waited for the two boys to run off and be noisy somewhere else.

Buttercup was quite proud of her coat. Some cats just had black, or ginger, or stripy tabby in their coat. But Buttercup had everything a kitten could have in hers. She had little marks of marmalade, touches of tabby and tortoiseshell, bits of black and brown and patches of white. She had heard the vet describe her coat as Tortie – which sounded very grand.

Buttercup yawned. *Perhaps I should sneak out to next door's garden and find a nice patch of lawn in the sun to have a nap*, she thought.

She poked her head out from under the table and, seeing that the boys weren't looking, she crept out from under the table and over to the kitchen door.

But just as Buttercup's nose touched the cat-flap, baby Lee caught sight of her. "Buttcup, Buttcup, Buttcup!" he screamed. He dropped the aeroplane, ran over and grabbed Buttercup roughly.

"Let go of her!" Freddie shouted, forgetting about his model aeroplane. "You're hurting Buttercup."

Buttercup was frightened. Lee was holding her tight and she was finding it hard to breathe.

"Let go!" Freddie shouted again. He reached out to grab Buttercup from Lee's

grasp. But this made the toddler hold on even tighter.

"You're hurting me!" Buttercup squealed. And she lashed out with her claws. To her dismay she saw red scratch marks make their way up Freddie's arm.

"What is all this noise?" Mrs Chapman asked, hurrying into the kitchen.

"Freddie won't let me have Buttcup!" Lee wailed.

"He's hurting her!" Freddie shouted.

Mrs Chapman shook her head, prised Buttercup out of Lee's pudgy fingers and put her gently on the floor. "You have to be gentle with her," she said firmly.

With relief Buttercup scurried away. She was about to escape to the garden when she caught sight of Freddie rubbing his arm. She went over to him and brushed her face against his legs. "Sorry," she miaowed, hoping he would understand. "I didn't mean to hurt you. I know you were only trying to help."

At that moment seven-year-old Clare ran into the kitchen. She saw the scratches on

Freddie's arm and, without waiting to hear what had happened, cried, "You've been teasing Buttercup, Freddie!" And she snatched Buttercup up and ran out of the room with her.

"You poor thing!" Clare said, as she ran upstairs and kicked open her bedroom door. "Come and play with me instead," she said, then put Buttercup down on the striped bedspread and sat down beside her.

Maybe Clare will let me have a rest, Buttercup thought. She walked slowly across the bed looking for a comfortable spot. Then, curling up against the slope of Clare's pillow, Buttercup closed her eyes.

"Buttercup," Clare said. "I've got a terrible secret that I have to share with someone . . ."

Slowly, Buttercup opened her eyes again. "You couldn't perhaps tell me later?" she began to miaow. But Clare had already started.

"Yesterday I trod on one of Freddie's computer games," she began. "And I broke it. But I didn't tell anyone. And now Freddie thinks Lee broke it and he's mad at him. And I'm scared to tell him it was me . . ."

Clare rambled on worrying about what to tell Freddie and biting her fingernails. Buttercup nuzzled against her trying to calm her down.

Suddenly Clare said, "I know what I could do. I could tell Freddie that I'll save up all my pocket money and buy him a new game. Do you think that's a good idea?"

"That's an excellent idea," Buttercup miaowed. And she licked Clare's hand. Clare threw herself back against the pillow and gave Buttercup a cuddle.

"Phew! I feel much better," she said. "Now, I've got another thing to ask you . . ."

But Buttercup was saved from hearing more by the sound of the doorbell followed by Mrs Chapman calling up the stairs, "Clare, Helen's here. It's time for your ballet class. Are you ready?"

"Coming," Clare shouted back. "I won't be a minute."

She ran round the room opening and

shutting drawers and cupboards looking for her ballet clothes. Finally, she bent down to give Buttercup a kiss on the top of her head whispering, "Let's talk some more when I get back." And she ran out of the room.

At last, Buttercup thought. I'm all alone. Now I really can have a nap. And she closed her eyes.

CRASH! The bedroom door flew open and five-year-old Jim raced in. "So there you are Buttercup!" he said. "I've been looking for you everywhere. I want you to come and see my Lego spaceship."

He lifted Buttercup off the bed and carried her downstairs explaining, "You're going to be the first cat in space."

"I don't want to be the first cat anywhere," Buttercup miaowed. "I just want to go to sleep."

Jim carried her into the sitting room, where Freddie was lying on the floor by the patio windows painting a picture. Buttercup would have liked to lie down quietly beside Freddie, but Jim plonked her down in the middle of a pile of plastic bricks.

"This is your spaceship," he told her. "Sit still and get ready for lift-off."

"It's uncomfortable," Buttercup miaowed, jumping off the bricks.

"Hey!" Jim ran after her. "You're going to be the first cat in space!"

"But I don't like sitting here," Buttercup miaowed. "Please hurry up and get started."

She sat as still as she could on the cold, uneven bricks while Jim shouted, "Ten, nine, eight, seven, six, five, four—"

"Stop shouting," Freddie yelled, looking up from his painting. "Can't you see I'm concentrating?"

Jim lowered his voice but continued his countdown. He zoomed around the room for a while, then he flopped down on the sofa. Using his hand like a microphone, he called, "Spaceship to mission control. We've arrived at Jupiter."

Good, thought Buttercup. If we've arrived, I can go. She leapt off the bricks and, seeing the patio doors were open a little, dashed towards the gap. Unfortunately, her route took her across Freddie's painting.

"Buttercup, come back," Jim shouted after her. "You're falling through space!"

"Not any more, she isn't," Freddie said, as he stood up angrily. "She's landed on my painting!"

Buttercup looked back to see what she'd done and saw a row of coloured pawprints across the wet painted paper. *Oh, no!* she thought. *I've upset poor Freddie – again!*

2

"Why don't you take your spaceship somewhere else?" Freddie shouted at Jim.

Good idea, Buttercup agreed.

Mrs Chapman rushed in to see what all the shouting was about and Buttercup fled out into the garden, looking for somewhere else to hide. At the far end of the lawn Buttercup spied a large white object beneath the apple tree. She padded up to explore – it was a sheet draped over the garden table. *Four-year-old Gilly must be playing house again,* she thought.

Buttercup gently pawed open the front flaps. Inside, a row of dolls sat silently on cushions.

Buttercup crept into the tent and tested out the cushions looking for the cosiest one. Then easing herself between two dolls, she curled up and closed her eyes.

"Teatime everyone!" Gilly's voice rang out, forcing Buttercup to open her eyes again. Gilly crawled into the tent carrying a tray with a toy teapot, milk jug and lots of teacups.

Gilly set down the tray and began to pour the pretend tea into a red plastic cup. She placed it in front of the first doll. "Here's a cup for you."

Then she turned to the second doll and placed a cup in front of her saying, "And here's one for you."

Buttercup lay very still, hoping that Gilly wouldn't notice her. And at first, the little girl was concentrating so hard on pouring the tea, that she didn't see Buttercup sitting amongst the dolls.

But then Buttercup was next in the row . . . "Hello, Buttercup," Gilly smiled. "I bet you're thirsty. Here's an extra big cup for you."

She placed a large blue cup in front of Buttercup who stared at it without moving. "I don't want tea," she mewed. "I just want to be left alone!"

Three cups of tea later, Buttercup made her escape while Gilly was preparing tea for a fourth round and wasn't looking. She crept out of the tent and dashed across the lawn, over to some large flowerpots. They stood next to a wall that ran in front of the basement flat. *If I lie down behind these flowerpots, hopefully nobody will find me*, she thought.

The stony ground wasn't as comfortable as a cushion or a blanket, but it was warm from the sun and Buttercup was so tired that she flopped down, stretched out and instantly began to doze off.

She was woken by the sound of footsteps coming up the stone steps. "So there you are, Buttercup," Gran said, bending down to stroke her. "I've got a special treat for you – fish pie."

Buttercup pricked up her ears. Tired as she was, she couldn't resist the idea of fish pie. She scampered down the steps after Gran into the basement flat.

Granddad was sitting at the kitchen table. When he saw Buttercup he put down his newspaper and spooned some of the leftover pie into Buttercup's bowl.

"You're going to love this, girl," he said. "It's one of Gran's best."

Buttercup had to agree. Gran's fish pie was always good. But this one was extra delicious. She purred loudly as she wolfed it down. *Now my tummy's full, I really will sleep well*, she thought happily.

She rubbed against Gran and Granddad's legs to say thank you, then walked towards the door. She was looking forward to going back to her spot in the sun, behind the flowerpots. "Oh don't run off yet," Gran said. "Come and sit on my lap, while we watch TV."

Buttercup really didn't want to. She loved Gran and Granddad – but they were both a bit deaf and had their TV on so loud, Buttercup just couldn't sleep.

Hours later, Buttercup crawled back into her basket, VERY tired. She'd had another exhausting day.

All the children were in bed and now, at last, it was her turn to get some rest. She closed her eyes. But as she was dozing off, Mr Chapman came into the kitchen to get a glass of water from the kitchen sink. "I have to get up really early tomorrow," he called to Mrs Chapman. "And if I sleep through the alarm again and am late for another meeting, I could lose my job this time!"

"And we're both such heavy sleepers . . ." said Mrs Chapman, sounding worried too.

Mr Chapman switched off the kitchen light and they went upstairs, discussing how they could make sure that he got up in time.

I'd better try and wake him in the morning, Buttercup thought. Although she was really tired, she knew it would be awful if Mr Chapman lost his job, and she always heard his alarm clock.

Buttercup closed her eyes again . . .

Beep, beep, beep, beep . . . Beep, beep, beep, beep . . .

From a long way off Buttercup heard a familiar sound. Slowly, she opened her eyes and looked around. It was still dark outside. Beep, beep, beep, beep . . . The noise continued. Then she remembered − Mr Chapman's alarm!

Yawning, she jumped out of her basket and ran lightly upstairs. *If he's awake, I can go straight back to bed again*, she thought.

But Mr Chapman wasn't awake. And neither was Mrs Chapman. They were both fast asleep − and Mr Chapman was snoring loudly.

Oh, dear! What shall I do? Buttercup wondered. She sprang up onto the bedside table, landing between a pile of books and the alarm clock. She reached out a paw towards Mr Chapman but she couldn't quite reach him.

As she tried to move closer, she knocked over the alarm clock. It crashed to the floor making a dreadful racket.

"What's that? What's going on?" Mr Chapman mumbled, rolling over and pushing back the covers. But instead of getting up, he opened his eyes for a second then closed them again and carried on snoring.

The clock had stopped beeping now. And Mr and Mrs Chapman kept sleeping. Buttercup couldn't believe it.

Well, there's only one thing left to do, Buttercup thought to herself. *I didn't want to do this, but I'm going to have to.* She sprang with all her might onto the hump in the duvet that was Mr Chapman. Then, she opened her mouth wide and yowled, "Wake up, Mr Chapman! It's time to get up!"

Mr Chapman jerked wide awake, and

quickly sat up. "Aargh! What was that?" He rubbed his eyes then saw Buttercup standing on the bed. "Buttercup!" he shouted, sounding annoyed. "What did you do that for?"

"Oh my goodness, look at the time!" Mrs Chapman said, waking up beside him and checking her watch. "You've got to get up. Thank goodness Buttercup came in when she did."

"Mum, mum," baby Lee called from next door. "Can I come and play?" He ran in and jumped onto his parents' bed. "Buttcup!" he said, reaching for Buttercup's tail.

"Oh no," Buttercup miaowed. "I knew this would happen if I started to miaow. Soon everyone will be awake and getting ready for school!"

She jumped off the bed, scampered down the stairs and out through the cat flap, mewing sadly to herself. *I love the Chapmans very much*, she thought, *but no matter how much a kitten loves her family, she still needs a little time to herself!*

Buttercup ran across the lawn and jumped onto the garden wall, then stretched out, miserably.

"What's the matter?"

Buttercup looked down to see a black-and-white cat peering up at her from the next garden. She'd seen him before and knew he was called Thin.

"Is something wrong?" Thin asked, walking over to the wall on his spindly legs. He jumped onto the wall and stretched his

skinny body out beside Buttercup.

"I'm so tired," Buttercup told him. "I haven't had a proper sleep because I'm just so busy looking after my family every day."

Buttercup told Thin about the day before. "I got caught up in a fight between baby Lee and Freddie," she said. "Then I listened to Clare's problems and travelled in a space ship with Jim. After that I had tea with Gilly and her dolls – and I sat with Gran and Granddad while they watched really loud TV. Then this morning I had to get up very early to wake up Mr Chapman. And though it's only morning, I'm already tired!" Buttercup finished.

Thin listened carefully, then thought for a while. "I know just the cat to help you out with your morning calls," he said.

"Who?" Buttercup asked.

"My mate Basil would make a brilliant alarm clock," Thin told her. "He howls so loudly that, wherever he is, he wakes half the street! And I know lots of other cats that would love to help you, too," Thin continued.

"Go on," said Buttercup, eager to hear more.

"For a start, there's Trouble the tabby, who adores playing with little children," miaowed Thin. "Then Marmalade Mimi is a wonderful listener – Clare would love her," he added. "I'm sure Silky the tortoiseshell would enjoy having tea with a kind little girl like Gilly," he miaowed. "And old Snowy is going a bit deaf himself – so if he had a cosy lap to sit on he'd snooze in front of a loud TV!"

Buttercup could hardly believe it. Her problems might be solved. "But how could I ever thank you?" she asked.

"Well . . ." Thin miaowed. "I've often smelled the most delicious fish pie smells coming from that basement flat . . ." he said. He licked his lips and continued, "It's ages since my owner has cooked fish pie – and it's my favourite!"

"Mine too!" said Buttercup. "I always get Gran and Granddad's leftovers – and you're more than welcome to share them!" She was so happy she leaned over and gave Thin a friendly nudge with her face. "Your friends sound perfect," she said. "But how will we find them?"

"Oh, they're here and there and round about," Thin replied. "But it shouldn't be too hard to track them down."

Buttercup jumped down from the wall. "Then let's go!" she miaowed.

3

Buttercup and Thin trotted along the road side by side. Whenever they heard a noise or saw a sudden movement, they hurried to take a look.

"There's someone in here," Buttercup miaowed, darting into a garden with an enormous flowerbed. "I think it's a tabby," she called to Thin.

But when they got closer the creature

dashed away and ran up a tree, waving its thick brushy tail. It was a squirrel.

"Never mind," miaowed Thin. "We'll soon be near the shops – and that's where I'm sure we'll find Basil."

They came to a busy road. Buttercup was a bit nervous and stayed close to Thin, who didn't seem worried by the noise and traffic at all. Then Buttercup noticed a familiar face. It was Elsie Jennings, the Bradmans' gran. She was wearing her big white coat. Buttercup remembered her wearing it sometimes when she called in to see the Bradmans on her way home from work.

Mrs Jennings was the local lollipop lady – she stood by the zebra crossing, holding up her sign to stop the traffic, while children crossed to get to school.

"Why Buttercup, is that you?" Mrs Jennings said, bending down to stroke her. "What are you doing so far from home? I hope you're not lost."

Buttercup purred, pleased to see Mrs Jennings again. She had known the old lady since the day she was born, but hadn't seen her since she'd gone to live with the Chapmans.

"I'm not lost," she miaowed, rubbing against Mrs Jenning's legs. "Thin and I are looking for his pals. He thinks they'll come to help me out at the Chapmans' house."

Just then some school children came along. While Mrs Jennings was busy helping them across the road, Buttercup and Thin made their escape. Soon they were round the corner and in the next street.

"Start exploring and listen carefully," Thin advised her. "Basil will be around here somewhere."

Buttercup walked along cautiously, sniffing the air. "I think I heard a noise down there," she miaowed, stopping at the entrance to a narrow alley that ran behind a row of shops.

Swiftly and silently, Thin and Buttercup raced towards the dustbins at the far end. All around the bins, there were plastic bags with their corners chewed and their contents spilling out.

They heard a lot of scampering. Then a dustbin lid clattered to the ground and Buttercup spotted a tail. But it wasn't a furry tail. It was a long, thin, hairless tail. "Look!" she hissed to Thin.

Just then the tail disappeared, and was replaced by a pointed face with twitching whiskers.

"It's a rat!" miaowed Thin. "I don't like rats. Nasty creatures – and they're not scared of me because I'm not much bigger than them! Let's go."

They raced back towards the street.

"Are you sure we'll find Basil round here?" Buttercup asked. She didn't like it very much in this strange part of town.

"Yes," miaowed Thin. "Just keep looking."

From round the corner they heard loud screeching sounds.

"That sounds like him," miaowed Thin.

They ran towards the noise, turned a corner and saw a large ginger cat, lying across the roof of a tumble-down shed.

They raced towards the shed. But as soon

as Basil saw two cats running towards him, he jumped down and hid in the narrow gap between the shed and the wall.

"Basil, come out, I want to ask you something," Buttercup miaowed when they caught up. But Basil stayed in hiding.

"Leave him to me," Thin miaowed. He jumped onto the shed and began to tell Basil all about Buttercup's problems.

Eventually, Basil came out from his hiding-place. "Pleased to meet you," he miaowed to Buttercup and went up to rub noses with her. "Sorry I ran away just now. Cats often pick fights with me and people usually throw things at me to scare me off. I'm not used to being invited anywhere. But I'd love to help if I can."

"That's great," miaowed Buttercup. "Why don't you come back to the Chapmans' house and see where I live?"

The three cats set off together, looking for Thin's other friends along the way. They came across a large house with a sign on the gate saying, BEWARE: GUARD DOG. A moment later they saw a large black dog running round the garden, snapping his jaws and chasing a small plump tabby.

"That's Trouble," miaowed Thin. "In trouble as usual."

Spotting them, Trouble gave up her game, raced over to the gate and squeezed through a gap, just as the dog's teeth snapped at her tail. "That was a close one!" she miaowed.

Thin introduced Buttercup to Trouble, who began walking back towards the Chapmans' house with them.

"You'll love my family," Buttercup miaowed. "And I'm sure they'll like you. There are five children and they're all very different and they all want loads of attention. They want to play and talk and—"

"They sound absolutely wonderful," a silky miaow interrupted.

The four cats looked up to see a tortoiseshell cat sitting in the branches of a cherry tree.

"Ah, Silky!" miaowed Thin. "We were looking for you!"

"Hello," Silky miaowed to Buttercup. "I couldn't help overhearing what you were saying. You're so lucky! I'm terribly fond of my owner, sweet old Mrs Tranter, but she never wants to play."

"Then why don't you come along too?" miaowed Buttercup.

"I'd love to," Silky purred, slithering down from her tree.

Now there were five of them, walking along as Buttercup told them about each member of the Chapman family. She was in the middle of describing Clare when there was a rustling in the bushes and two more cats sprang out in front of them. One was a huge marmalade cat and the other was elderly-looking and a rather grubby white.

"And here are our last two friends!" miaowed Thin, happily. "Marmalade Mimi and old Snowy."

"I'd just love to sit and listen to Clare's problems all day long!" agreed Mimi. "It's ages since anybody talked to me. The children in my family have all grown up and moved away. I'd love to help you out."

Thin yowled their plan as loudly as he could into deaf old Snowy's ear. "Gran and Granddad Chapman sound just like my kind of people," he miaowed in a deep croaky voice. "Lead the way!"

Buttercup was beginning to feel really hopeful. All Thin's friends were keen to help. She trotted along the street with her six motley helpers. And what a sight they were – marmalade, tabby, tortoiseshell, black-and-white – together they made up all the colours in Buttercup's coat!

When they arrived at the Chapmans' house, Buttercup suggested that they all wait for a while behind the garden shed. "I'm going to introduce you one at a time," she explained. "I'll be as quick as I can."

Then she turned to Trouble. "Follow me," she miaowed. And she led her to where Jim was playing with his spaceship on the lawn.

"Buttercup, you're just in time for take-off," Jim called out happily. "We're going to Mars, this time!"

He lifted Buttercup in his arms and placed her on the Lego® bricks. Trouble jumped up beside her. "Great!" said Jim. "Two cats in space."

He zoomed around the garden, yelling instructions to Mission Control. And whenever he shouted, Trouble stood up and miaowed along with him. When Buttercup crept silently away, Jim hardly seemed to notice.

Buttercup hurried back to her helpers. "This way," she told Silky, leading her across the garden into the tent. "Let's snuggle down between the dolls," she miaowed. "Gilly will be on her way soon with the tea tray."

Gilly crawled into the tent. "Well done, Buttercup," she said when she caught sight of Silky. "You've brought along a friend." And she began to pour out cups of tea.

Silky drank hers and miaowed for more. And Gilly didn't seem to mind at all when Buttercup slipped out leaving Silky on the cushions, purring merrily.

"Come with me," Buttercup miaowed to Mimi next. The big tortoiseshell cat followed her into the house and up the stairs to Clare's room.

"Ssh," Buttercup warned, when they passed baby Lee's bedroom and saw that he was asleep. "You don't want to wake baby Lee. He picked me up and almost squashed me yesterday."

They scurried into Clare's room and jumped onto her bed.

"Oh, how lovely, there's two of you for me to talk to," Clare smiled and immediately began to stroke them both. "I'm so pleased you're here," she told them. "Because I've got a big problem. Yesterday at school someone threw something at the teacher and when she turned round she thought it was me. But it wasn't me. I think I know who it was but . . ."

Clare twirled her hair around her fingers and carried on talking. Mimi purred and miaowed and watched Clare's every movement with her large green eyes. She was so happy to be stroked again and to have someone wanting to talk to her.

When Buttercup slithered off the bed and slipped out of the room, Clare didn't seem bothered at all.

"Now it's your turn," Buttercup yowled as loudly as she could into Snowy's ear. She led him and Thin across the lawn and down to the basement where Gran and Granddad were sitting reading.

"Hello, Buttercup, I suppose you want some more leftovers," Gran said, getting slowly to her feet.

Bending stiffly, Gran put down a saucer of shepherd's pie. Buttercup's mouth watered. It was her second favourite after fish pie!

She took a few mouthfuls then miaowed for Thin and Snowy to join her.

"Hey, you naughty cats, go away!" Gran scolded. But when she saw the longing in Thin's eyes and saw how old and stiff Snowy was, she said, "I think we've found a couple of new friends, Granddad."

Buttercup left them to it and raced back to Basil, who was sitting patiently soaking up the sun.

"If you don't mind, I'll be off now," he
told her, standing up and stretching. "But
I'll be happy to lend a hand when anyone
needs an early morning call," he promised.
"You know where to find me."

"Thanks," miaowed Buttercup and she
watched him slink away.

"Hey, come back," a voice called from
nearby. "I haven't finished my picture
yet."

Freddie was lying on the grass with his pens
and pencils and a sheet of paper in front of

him. He was holding up a half-finished drawing of Basil.

Basil stopped in his tracks. "Don't worry," he miaowed to Buttercup. "I'd be happy to stay a little longer. After all, nobody has ever wanted to paint my picture before." He walked back and sat down in front of Freddie again.

Buttercup strolled slowly round the garden. *Is it really possible that everyone is happy and I have some time to myself?* she wondered.

She went and lay down in her favourite spot beyond the apple tree, where the grass was warmed by the sun. Curling her tail around her, Buttercup closed her eyes and breathed in gently.

At last, thanks to Thin and her other wonderful new friends, she was free to do what she'd wanted to do ever since she arrived at the Chapman house. She was free to take some very long naps!

Weed

1

Weed, the tiniest of Bracken's kittens, was snoozing beside her mum. She felt warm breath on her face and opened one eye. A strange-looking woman was staring down at her with big brown eyes, ringed in black. Her mouth was a rather scary bright red.

I don't like the look of her! Weed decided. She squeezed both eyes shut and wriggled closer to Bracken, hoping the woman would go away.

Weed was the last of Bracken's litter to be born, and a small, scraggy, quiet little thing. Now she was the only kitten left in the basket in the Bradmans' kitchen in Liberty Street. All her brothers and sisters had found new homes.

"Let's have a look at you then!"

Suddenly Weed felt a bony hand with long sharp nails yank her away from the safety and warmth of her mum. She felt herself being whooshed through the air and opened her eyes wide in fright. She was being held by the scary woman!

The familiar, cosy scent of Bracken was replaced by the overpowering smell of the woman's strong perfume. "Oh, I can't breathe," Weed spluttered. "Atishoo!"

"Oh, yuk!" The woman's red mouth twisted in horror as Weed sneezed in her face. She let go of the kitten.

Weed felt herself falling through the air. "Help!" she miaowed.

A pair of large warm hands caught her. Phew! Then she felt herself being lifted upwards again. Weed turned her head to see who was holding her now. It was a man, with smiling blue eyes. "Let's have a look at you then," he said in a deep voice. Weed blinked up at him. He didn't seem so bad, she thought.

The man cupped her in one hand and with the other picked up a white stick that was glowing at one end. He sucked on it, then breathed out a puff of white smelly smoke all over Weed. She coughed and spluttered, "Oh no, I really can't breathe now!"

The man hurriedly tried to pass Weed to a girl that was standing next to the scary woman. But the girl held her hands away.

"No, I don't want to hold her," she said, sulkily. "I don't want that kitten – I want a really pretty one."

The man sighed and put Weed back down in the basket, next to Bracken.

Phew! Weed thought. *What a relief! I'd much rather stay here with the Bradmans.* She huddled as close as she could to her mum, curled into a tight ball in the basket and closed her eyes.

"Sorry. Your kitten isn't exactly what we're looking for," said the man, puffing on his cigarette as he followed his wife and daughter out of the room.

As Mrs Bradman saw the family out, the girl was saying, "I don't want a kitten like that. I want a really pretty one . . ."

"Thank goodness they've gone," Tom Bradman said as the front door was shut. "They didn't seem very nice."

"Poor Weed," said Ellie, looking at Weed, snuggled up next to Bracken. "What are we going to do with you?"

When people had come to choose one of Bracken's kittens they'd chosen their kitten for its lovely coat, or pretty face or cheeky personality. But Weed didn't have any of these attractions. And so far, no one had wanted her.

"Don't worry, someone, somewhere will want her," said Mrs Jennings, Ellie's gran. Mrs Jennings lived just down the road in a garden flat and was always popping in and out of the Bradmans' house. She'd been there when Bracken had given birth to her nine kittens and had always had a soft spot for little Weed. She was also the local lollipop lady.

Hearing Mrs Jennings' voice, Weed opened her eyes. She loved Gran. "I wish you wanted me," she mewed.

"I hope you're right, Gran," said Ellie, frowning. "But we have to make sure Weed goes to exactly the right kind of home. We can't let her go just anywhere, to get rid of her."

"Of course not," Mrs Bradman said, putting an arm round her daughter. "You know we'd never do that."

All the Bradmans were worried that Weed wouldn't find another home. But Weed wasn't worried at all. She didn't mind how long she stayed with the Bradmans. The longer the better, as far as she was concerned! Now that her brothers and sisters had moved away, she got to be close to her mum all day long and had loads of attention from the Bradmans.

The doorbell rang.

"That'll be the Taylors," Mrs Bradman said. "They sounded really nice on the telephone." Gran went with her to the door to meet them.

A few moments later, three children pushed their way into the kitchen. They all raced towards the cat basket.

"I'm going to see the kitten first," one of the boys said.

"But I'm going to hold her first," said the other.

"No, I am!" shrieked the girl. "Mum said I could be first!"

Oh no, am I going to be pulled to bits now? Weed wondered, looking up at the squabbling children. She tried to wriggle under Bracken, but three pairs of hands reached out for her at once and she didn't have a chance. They pushed and pulled the basket, each trying to grab hold of Weed. Bracken yowled in alarm.

"I've got her," the older boy shouted.

"No, you haven't. I've got her," said the other.

"But I'm supposed to be holding her," the girl screeched. "Give her to me!"

For a few seconds Weed was crushed against a woolly blue sweater. Then her face was squashed into a red anorak. And after a while a pair of sticky hands held her against a white cotton sweatshirt.

"I can't see what she looks like," the girl wailed.

"Let go and I'll show you," the older boy shouted.

"No, you let go and I'll show you both," the younger boy screamed.

"Put me back. Please put me back," Weed miaowed, squirming to get free. She caught sight of a horrified Ellie and Tom, then a man and woman came into the kitchen.

Mrs Bradman and Gran followed them in. "Oh, my goodness!" they cried, as they saw the Taylor children grabbing Weed – in between punching, slapping and pulling one another's hair!

"Daniel, Sam, Kate!" said Mrs Taylor in a high, agitated voice. "Do calm down!" she pleaded.

"Mum! You said I could be first!" Kate cried, red in the face.

"No, you said I could," the older boy complained.

"It's my turn, Mum!" the younger boy whined.

"Leave the children to sort it out for themselves," said the rather sour-faced Mr Taylor to his wife.

Just then, Mr Bradman, who had been digging the garden, hurried into the kitchen to see what was going on. He had heard the commotion through the open kitchen window.

Lottie, the Bradmans' dog, bounded in after him, barking. She rushed up to the biggest boy who was clutching Weed, and pulled at his anorak.

"Hey, let go of my kid, you vicious dog!" Mr Taylor shouted. He swung a foot to kick out at Lottie. The Golden Retriever managed to dodge the blow and carried on barking loudly.

Mr Bradman had seen enough. "I think it's time we put the kitten back with her mother, don't you?" he told the Taylor children calmly but firmly. And he quickly lifted Weed out of the older boy's hands and set her back beside Bracken.

Then he turned to Mr and Mrs Taylor. "I'm afraid there's been a mistake," he said. "Weed isn't in need of a new home after all." He ushered them out of the kitchen and towards the front door.

"Well, that was a waste of time, wasn't it?" Mr Taylor snapped angrily at his wife.

"Let's just go!" she snapped back.

"Mum, you said we were getting a new kitten," the older boy whined.

"You promised we'd get one today," his younger brother joined in.

"I want that kitten — and I want it now!" Kate squealed as the front door banged shut behind them.

Back in her basket Weed was shivering

with fright. "Oh, that was awful," she mewed, as Bracken gently licked her to try and calm her down.

"There's no way we could ever let Weed go to a difficult family like that," Mrs Bradman said. "They really upset her." She shook her head. "And Mrs Taylor sounded so nice and polite on the phone! What a shock to find out what they were really like!"

Gran went over to the cat basket and bent down to stroke Weed.

"They almost pulled me apart," Weed mewed up at her.

"There, there, little one," Gran whispered softly. "Don't you worry. Gran won't let you go to a new home unless it's absolutely perfect."

"I wish I didn't have to go anywhere at all," Weed miaowed back.

2

Later that evening, when Gran had gone home and the Bradmans were chatting in the kitchen, the doorbell rang.

"I'll get it," Tom said, leaping up to open the door.

"I'm Mrs Jones and this is my daughter Alice," a woman's voice said. "We heard that you were looking for a home for a kitten and we'd love to see it. I hope you don't mind us dropping round like this. Can we come in now?"

"I think so," Tom said. Then he shouted through to the kitchen, "There are some people here to see Weed. Is it all right if I bring them in?"

"That's fine," Mrs Bradman replied and she hurried out to meet them.

Weed looked up from the basket. She felt anxious. *I don't want any more people staring and holding me*, she thought, unhappily.

She could hear voices and footsteps coming down the hall. Just before Tom and Mrs Bradman and the visitors came into the kitchen, Weed skipped out of her basket and ran through the arch to the adjoining sitting room. Flattening her tummy against the floor, she crawled under the sofa.

Bracken saw her go and so did Ellie. But neither of them did anything to stop her. Mr Bradman, who was busily folding up the newspaper he'd been reading, hadn't noticed.

"This is Weed," Tom said, leading Alice Jones towards the basket. Then he stopped, surprised. "Oh! She was here a minute ago. Did anyone see where Weed went?" he asked.

Ellie shook her head, keeping her fingers crossed behind her back.

"She can't have gone far," Mr Bradman said.

Tom and his mum and dad began to walk around the room, calling Weed. Ellie joined in, not wanting to give the game away. "Come here, Weed," she called. "There's someone here to see you."

But I don't know if I want to see them, Weed thought, staying where she was, in her hiding-place under the sofa. She could hear everything that was going on in the kitchen.

"I can't wait to see this kitten," Alice said excitedly. "I hope we can find her soon. I'm longing to hold her."

"Alice has been wanting a kitten for ages," Mrs Jones explained.

Alice sounds quite nice, Weed thought, slithering forward far enough to peep out from her hiding-place and take a look at the visitors.

First she saw the back of Alice's white trainers and green tracksuit bottoms. Looking up, she saw that Alice had long brown hair. Then Alice turned round and Weed saw her friendly face.

She looks really nice, Weed thought. Almost as nice as Ellie. She crawled back under the sofa to think. *If I really do have to go, perhaps it might be all right to go and live with a girl like her.*

Meanwhile, Mr Bradman and Tom began searching the sitting-room.

"Weed, where are you?" Mr Bradman called. "There's nothing to be frightened of."

Weed wasn't quite sure yet and stayed where she was.

Mr Bradman lifted up the cushions on the sofa and looked under the piles of newspapers and magazines that littered the room.

Tom opened and shut cupboard doors. "Come on, Weed. Everything's OK. Come on out," he called.

Ellie came into the room and, on her hands and knees, looked under the sofa. "Weed, I think you might like Alice. Perhaps you should come and meet her," she whispered.

Weed crept a little closer. *If everyone thinks Alice is OK, then perhaps I should trust them,* she thought. "Maybe you're right," she mewed in her tiniest voice.

She had just decided to crawl out to take a proper look at Alice when Mrs Bradman asked, "Have you got any other pets, Alice?"

"Yes," Alice replied, grinning. "I've got loads."

"Oh," Ellie said, going back into the kitchen. "How many?"

Weed watched Alice hold up her fingers and begin to count. "I've got two hamsters and three guinea pigs, four rabbits and two bantam hens that lay eggs. Then I've got a pet snake and some fish and I've got a lovely cuddly chinchilla that hops about all over the place . . ."

As Alice listed all her pets, the Bradmans stopped looking for Weed. Lottie, who had been about to leap forward and sniff around the sofa so that they would know where Weed was hiding, backed away and sat in her corner by the door.

Meanwhile, Weed crept right back under the sofa. *I don't want to live with lots of other pets*, she thought worriedly. *I might not like them and they might not like me!*

"That's all of them," Alice said. "But I don't have a kitten and I'm simply longing for one."

"Well, I'm afraid we seem to have lost our kitten," said Mrs Bradman. She looked at Mrs Jones. "I'm so sorry . . . Um . . . we'll give you a ring when we find her."

A couple of minutes later, Weed heard the front door close and Mrs Bradman came back into the kitchen. "With all those other pets to look after, Alice wouldn't have much time for Weed," she said.

Mr Bradman nodded. "It's a pity because she's a nice little girl," he said, sitting back down at the kitchen table.

"Yes, but Weed deserves someone who has plenty of time to give her lots of love and attention," Ellie said fiercely.

Now that it was safe again, Weed crawled

out from under the sofa and scuttled into the kitchen.

"So there you are," said Tom. "Where have you been hiding?"

Weed rubbed up against Ellie's legs. "Thank you for helping me," she miaowed. Then she scampered over to the basket and happily snuggled up beside Bracken.

Several days passed. Nobody phoned about a kitten and nobody came to the door looking for one.

"Do you think we should put up some notices?" Tom suggested one morning at breakfast. "I could ask Angie and Steve if I could put one in their shop window." Tom was a paperboy. Early every morning, he delivered newspapers for the shop on the corner of Liberty Street. It was run by Angie and Steve, who had given a home to Jet, another of Bracken's kittens.

"Maybe," said Mr Bradman, sipping his tea. "But it seems as though everyone who wants a kitten round here has already got one."

Ellie was buttering her toast. She listened, but didn't join in the conversation. She had grown more and more fond of Bracken's last little kitten. She dreaded the day when she would have to say goodbye to her.

Ellie was still thinking of Weed as she walked to school.

As always, Gran was standing at the zebra crossing in her big white coat. She held up her lollipop-shaped sign to stop the traffic while children crossed the road. As she walked back to the pavement, she noticed Ellie.

"Morning, love," she said, giving her a hug. "You look very glum! What's the matter?"

"It's Weed, Gran," Ellie sighed.

"Oh, have you found a home for her then?" her gran asked, looking a little bit upset.

"No, that's the problem," said Ellie. "Mind you, I don't really want her to go at all."

Her gran smiled. "Neither do I," she confided.

"But there haven't been that many people interested in Weed," Ellie said, standing on one foot and then the other. "I'm scared that we'll have to give Weed to someone who's not quite right." She looked at her gran. "Can't you think of anyone who would make a good owner for our Weed, Gran?"

"Not off the top of my head," said Gran. "But I'll try."

That afternoon, as Ellie was coming in from school, the telephone rang. Ellie picked it up. It was a Mr Clarke. "I've heard you've got a kitten that needs a home," he said in a friendly voice. "And she sounds just right for my nephews."

"Could you bring them round to meet her?" Ellie asked.

"I don't think that's necessary," Mr Clarke replied. "*I* can decide if she's right for the boys."

Ellie wasn't happy about that. She called her mum to the phone and was relieved when she heard her firmly telling Mr Clarke, "But we have to see if the boys are right for our kitten."

Reluctantly, Mr Clarke agreed to call round that evening with the boys. But when the doorbell rang at seven o'clock, he stood alone on the doorstep.

"Oh, where are your nephews?" Ellie asked in surprise, when she opened the door.

"I'm afraid they were busy tonight," he explained. "But I thought I'd come by anyway as you were expecting me. I'd love to see the kitten."

Ellie showed Mr Clarke into the kitchen.

He went across to Bracken's basket and picked Weed up. "What a tiny little thing you are," he said, smiling.

Weed sat in the palm of his large hands and looked up at his friendly round face and warm brown eyes. She felt safe in his big, strong hands and didn't struggle or try to jump back into her basket. *Perhaps you're not too bad*, she thought.

Mr and Mrs Bradman were surprised and pleased. Tom grinned and Ellie, who had been pacing up and down since Mr Clarke had phoned, began to relax.

"Why don't you join us for a cup of tea?" Mrs Bradman suggested. "And tell us about your nephews."

Mr Clarke sat at the table with Weed on his lap, describing the boys. "Simon and Jake are seven and eight years old and they're lively young lads," he said. "With lots of energy."

"Have they got any other pets?" Ellie asked, passing him the milk.

"Thanks. No, but they've been wanting one for a long time. They'd love a little kitten like this." Mr Clarke helped himself to the sugar and stirred his tea. He looked down at Weed who was licking his hand.

"If the boys are like you," Weed miaowed, "I suppose I wouldn't mind living with them."

Mr and Mrs Bradman continued to chat to Mr Clarke. Everyone was smiling and beginning to feel that perhaps they'd found the right home for Weed at last. Mr Clarke sipped his tea and stroked Weed affectionately.

Then Mrs Bradman said, "Of course, we would still have to meet the boys and their parents before we could let Weed go."

"But I really wanted the kitten as a surprise," Mr Clarke said, looking disappointed. Then he sighed. "To tell you the truth," he said, "the boys have been getting into a little bit of trouble lately. I thought having a kitten might help to calm them down – stop them being so rough—"

"What kind of trouble?" Mr Bradman asked seriously.

"Well, they smashed a window – and they threw stones at the neighbour's dog," Mr Clarke admitted, looking embarrassed.

Over in the cat basket Bracken's fur began to stand on end. Lottie, who had been dozing on her blanket, pricked up her ears and growled.

Ellie stared in disbelief at Mr Clarke and shook her head vigorously at her mother. *What if Mr Clarke was wrong? What if having a kitten didn't calm his nephews down – and they were cruel to sweet little Weed? No! They couldn't risk it!*

Weed hadn't liked what she'd heard either. She looked across at Bracken and began to mew. "I think he's all right – but I don't like the sound of his nephews!"

Just then the telephone rang and Ellie ran into the hall to answer it. A few moments later, she let out a happy shriek. Then she called Mrs Bradman to the phone.

Everyone in the kitchen stood around, looking uncomfortable. Then Mrs Bradman and Ellie came back in. Ellie was smiling widely.

"I'm afraid there's been a change of plan, Mr Clarke," Mrs Bradman said. "Someone else, already interested in Weed, is going to give her a home."

3

"Well, that's a shame," said Mr Clarke, looking disappointed. He put Weed back down in the cat basket next to Bracken, who pulled her kitten close and began to give her a wash.

"Thank goodness!" Bracken purred. "I didn't want you to go and live with those two nasty boys, either!"

"I suppose I'll have to think of something

else to keep those two young rascals out of mischief," Mr Clarke continued.

"I think that would be best," replied Mr Bradman.

Mr Clarke finished his tea and let Mrs Bradman show him out.

"Well done, Mum," said Tom, as she came back into the kitchen. "That was a clever excuse."

"It's not a excuse — it's true!" Ellie said, happily. She went over and picked Weed up, cuddling the kitten against her chest. "Someone does want you, little Weed."

"Who?" asked Tom and Mr Bradman, surprised.

"Yes, who?" Weed miaowed.

Ellie smiled at her mum, who smiled back at her. "We're not telling, just yet," she said mysteriously. "Just wait and see."

"But why do we have to wait?" Tom asked. "It's not fair. Come on, Ellie, tell us."

"You'll find out tomorrow night," his sister replied. "Promise!"

★ ★ ★

That evening Weed curled up close beside Bracken in the cat basket. *Is this really the last evening I'll spend here?* she wondered.

She looked around the Bradmans' untidy kitchen and remembered all the times she'd spent there. First there was the crowded basket with all her noisy brothers and sisters fighting to get close to their mum. Then, one by one, the other kittens had left for their new homes – until she was the only one left. Since then, Weed had enjoyed having a special time, with Bracken all to herself, and lots of attention from the Bradman family and Lottie, their dog. *But where am I going to now?* she wondered. *Which home has Ellie decided is right for me?*

Weed thought long and hard about all the people who had been to see her. None of them seemed right to her. *Well, it can't be the Walkers, because they didn't want me*, she decided. *And surely it's not the Taylors who were so angry with each other they almost pulled me apart? And it can't be Alice because everyone said she had too many pets already . . . So who can it be?*

Weed stretched and yawned. She was too tired to think about it any more. She snuggled into Bracken's fur and closed her eyes for her last precious night's sleep beside her mum.

The next day, before Tom left for his paper round, he dashed across to say goodbye to Weed as he did every morning. But this time he lifted her right out of the basket and gave her a kiss on the nose. "It's not going to be the same without you," he whispered. "I'm really going to miss your sweet little face."

"I'm going to miss you too," Weed miaowed.

After Tom had gone, Lottie bounded over and asked Weed if she wanted to go and play in the garden. Since it had taken such a long time to find Weed a new home, she'd had her injections and for the last couple of weeks had been allowed to go outside.

"Oh, yes please!" Weed miaowed, thinking it would help to take her mind off things.

She wriggled out through the cat flap and scampered across the grass.

Then she hid behind a bush and waited for the Golden Retriever to bark for someone to let her out.

It didn't take Lottie long to find Weed, once Ellie had opened the back door for her. She chased Weed through the flowerbeds, yapping gently at her back legs.

Weed let Lottie catch her up and they both collapsed on the grass, panting.

"Who am I going to play with in the garden when you've gone?" Lottie barked. "Your mum has never really liked playing with me."

"I don't know," mewed Weed sadly, reaching over to lick her friend's nose.

When Weed climbed back through the cat flap, Mr Bradman was just leaving for work. She twined round his legs, purring.

Mr Bradman stroked the top of her head. "The house is going to feel a bit empty without you, little one," he said sadly.

"You've been with us so long, we've all got used to having you here."

But Ellie was cheerful as she left for school. "See you later, Weed," she called over her shoulder. "And don't worry — everything's going to be all right."

"I wish you'd tell me where I'm going," Weed miaowed. But Ellie just grinned at her mum and left.

"Hello, Gran," said Tom as he opened the door that evening. Gran always came round to dinner on a Tuesday. "Did you hear about Weed? She's got a new owner — but Mum and Ellie won't tell us who it is yet!"

"Is that right?" said Gran, giving her Tom a kiss. "I'm sure we'll find out soon enough," she said, following Tom into the kitchen.

Everyone sat at the kitchen table as Mrs Bradman served up a big bowl of pasta.

"OK. Now I'm going to tell you about Weed's new home," Ellie said, grinning. She took a deep breath and looked around the table.

Everyone waited expectantly. Lottie moved closer and put her head on one side to listen and Bracken sat up in her basket. Weed stopped washing herself. *Here goes*, she thought, swivelling her ears forward so she wouldn't miss anything.

"Well," Ellie began. "Weed's new home is really close to here and there aren't any other pets. It's got a nice garden and a very loving owner, who says that Weed can come home and visit Bracken and all of us whenever she wants to."

"That sounds good," Weed miaowed. Bracken purred and gave her a motherly lick. Lottie barked her approval, too.

"That sounds great," Mr Bradman said. "But where exactly is it?"

"And how can you be so sure it's right for Weed?" Tom added insistently.

"And who is it?" Weed miaowed.

"I know it's right, because I know Weed's new home very well," Ellie explained. "We all do!" she laughed. "And we all know the owner as well as anyone in our family."

"That's impossible!" Tom exploded.

"It isn't," Gran interrupted. "Because . . . it's me!"

"That's why I didn't tell you yesterday," Ellie continued. "Because I wanted Gran to be here, too."

But nobody was listening to Ellie any more. The whole table had erupted as they all jumped up to give Gran a hug and a kiss.

"Hurrah!" shouted Tom.

"Fantastic!" said Mr Bradman clapping his

hands. "I can't believe the answer was right under our noses all the time."

Thoroughly excited by the celebrations, Lottie barked and leaped up at everyone, wanting to join in. Bracken jumped out of her basket, miaowing loudly. As for Weed, she trembled with excitement. Then she skipped out of the basket after her mum, and skidded across to Gran.

Everyone looked down at the little kitten.

"How do you feel about coming to live with me then, little one?" Gran said. She reached out a hand and tickled Weed under the chin.

Purring with happiness, Weed jumped up onto Gran's lap. She looked up at her new owner's kind, friendly face. "The only place I would ever really want to live, other than here," she miaowed, "is down the road with you!"

More titles in the Nine Lives Trilogy by

LUCY DANIELS

0 340 73619 4	GINGER, NUGMEG AND CLOVE	£3.50	❑
0 340 73620 8	EMERALD, AMBER AND JET	£3.50	❑

All Hodder Children's books are available at your local bookshop or newsagent, or can be ordered direct from the publisher. Just tick the titles you want and fill in the form below. Prices and availability subject to change without notice.

Hodder Children's Books, Cash Sales Department, Bookpoint, 39 Milton Park, Abingdon, OXON, OX14 4TD, UK. If you have a credit card you may order by telephone, our call team would be delighted to take your order by telephone. Our direct line is *01235 400414* (lines open 9.00 am–6.00 pm Monday to Saturday, 24 hour message answering service). Alternatively you can send a fax on *01235 400454.*

Or please enclose a cheque or postal order made payable to Bookpoint Ltd to the value of the cover price and allow the following for postage and packing: UK & BFPO – £1.00 for the first book, 50p for the second book, and 30p for each additional book ordered up to a maximum charge of £3.00. OVERSEAS & EIRE – £2.00 for the first book, £1.00 for the second book, and 50p for each additional book.

Name ....

Address ....

....

....

If you would prefer to pay by credit card, please complete:
Please debit my Visa/Access/Diner's Card/American Express (delete as applicable) card no:

Signature ....

Expiry Date ....